Dear Rama and Raja,
I miss you!
Please come
for a visit.

Love,
Auntie Rwanda

A. Rwanda
AFRICA

Rama and Raja
ASIA

Elephants Aloft

Written by

KATHI APPELT

Illustrated by

KEITH BAKER

Voyager Books
Harcourt Brace & Company
SAN DIEGO   NEW YORK   LONDON

For Katherine

—K. A.

For Babar and Celeste
and all the travelers
in the world

—K. B.

Requests for permission to make copies of any part of the work
should be mailed to: Permissions Department,
Harcourt Brace & Company, 6277 Sea Harbor Drive,
Orlando, Florida 32887-6777.

First Voyager Books edition 1997
Voyager Books is a registered trademark of Harcourt Brace & Company.

Library of Congress Cataloging-in-Publication Data
Appelt, Kathi, 1954–
Elephants aloft/Kathi Appelt; illustrations by Keith Baker.
p. cm.
"Voyager Books."
Summary: Using prepositions, relates the adventures of two elephants
as they travel to Africa to visit their Auntie Rwanda.
ISBN 0-15-225384-X
ISBN 0-15-201556-6 pb
[1. Elephants—Fiction. 2. English language—Prepositions—Fiction.]
I. Baker, Keith, 1953– ill. II. Title.
PZ7.A6455El 1993
[E]—dc20 92-4231

F E D C B A

Printed in Singapore

The illustrations in this book were done in Liquitex acrylics on illustration board.
The text and display type was set in ITC Goudy Sans Bold.
Composition by Thompson Type, San Diego, California
Color separations by Bright Arts, Ltd., Singapore
Printed and bound by Tien Wah Press, Singapore
This book was printed on Leykam recycled paper, which contains more than 20 percent
postconsumer waste and has a total recycled content of at least 50 percent.
Production supervision by Stanley Redfern and Jane Van Gelder
Designed by Michael Farmer

In

above

beside

through

between

behind

across

below

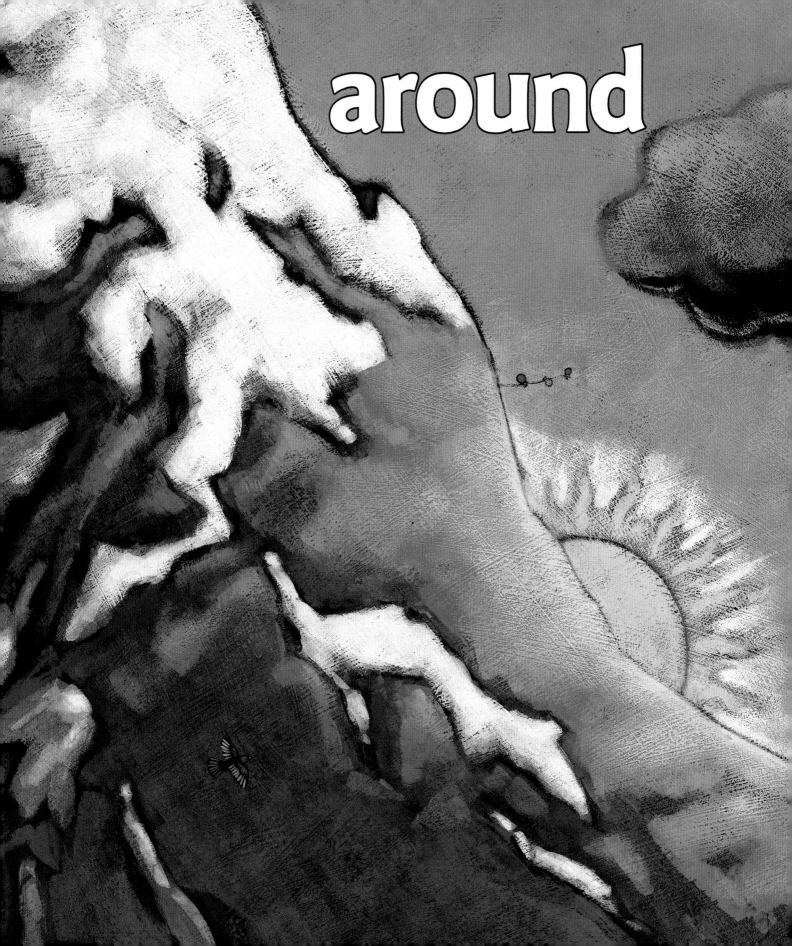

around

under

beyond

over

out

and into the arm

of Auntie Rwanda.